SUPER SILLY SCHOOL POEMS

poems by
David Greenberg

pictures by
Liza Woodruff

Orchard Books • New York • An Imprint of Scholastic Inc.

To Susan, My luminous sweetheart wife, Love, Your Duvy
—D.G.

For Jean, Kara, and Michelle
—L.W.

Text copyright © 2014 by David Greenberg
Illustrations copyright © 2014 by Liza Woodruff

Library of Congress Cataloging-in-Publication Data
Greenberg, David (David T.), author.
Super silly school poems / poems by David Greenberg ; pictures by Liza Woodruff.
pages cm
ISBN 978-0-545-47981-3
1. Schools—Juvenile poetry. I. Woodruff, Liza, illustrator. II. Title.
PS3557.R37828S87 2014
811.54—dc23
2013035035

10 9 8 7 6 5 4 3   14 15 16 17 18

Printed in the U.S.A. 40
First printing, July 2014
The display type was set in Chauncy Decaf.
The illustrations are watercolor and colored pencil.

Table of Contents

Introduction 4

Something You Forgot 6

My Teacher Is a Mind Reader 8

Belch! Giggle! Click! Crash! 10

My Dog Ate My Homework 12

A Lovely Place to Sleep 13

The Extremely Modern School Bathroom 14

Better Than Baseball 16

The Tastiest Taste 18

It's Time for Homework 20

Snakes on the Loose! 22

Teacher Sighting 24

What's for Lunch? 26

The Worst Smell of All 28

You Really Wanted to Do Your Homework, but... 30

Show-and-Tell Surprise 31

Final Word 32

Introduction

Here's a book of poems
All about your school
Do you think that they'll be boring?
Do you think that they'll be cool?

Here's a book of poems
You're certainly allowed
To read them to yourself
Or shout each one out loud

Here's a book of poems
Read them to a bug
Read them to your dog
While stretched out on the rug

Read the poems at dinner
Under blankets on your bed
Read them in a bubble bath
Just read them — go ahead!

Something You Forgot

You remembered to bring your art project
And the markers you just bought
Of course, you remembered your backpack
But there's something you forgot

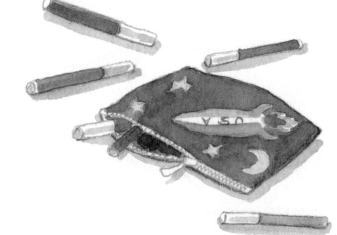

You remembered to bring the video game
That you very recently got
You remembered to bring your lunch money
But there's something you forgot

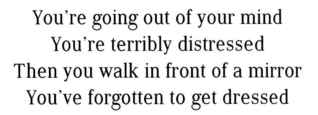

You know you've forgotten something
You fidget and you fret
You remembered to brush your teeth
But what did you forget?

You're going out of your mind
You're terribly distressed
Then you walk in front of a mirror
You've forgotten to get dressed

My Teacher Is a Mind Reader

If you as much as whisper
    Your teacher is aware

Scribble on your desk?
You haven't got a prayer

She knows you're eating candy
When she hasn't even looked

And if you're chewing gum
Dude, your goose is cooked!

Belch! Giggle! Click! Crash!

A pencil sharpener sharpening
A squeaking seat
A belch and a giggle
Tapping feet

An eraser rubbing
A clicking pen
Rolling the pen across the desk
Clicking it again

Crumpling paper
Dropping it in the trash
A student tipping backward
A giant CRASH

Swish

AAAAAAAAAAA

C R A S H

Pages flipping
Water fountain dripping
Blowing noses
Packs unzipping

flip flip flip

drip drip drip

PUSH

Your teacher said it's "Quiet Time"
So you only hear the noise
Of extremely quiet girls
And extremely quiet boys

HONK
HONK

ZZZZIIIIIIIIIPPPP
NNZZ

My Dog Ate My Homework

More than crunchy biscuits
More than juicy meat
Homework is the food
That doggies love to eat

A Lovely Place to Sleep

Take every coat in class
Make a giant heap
Burrow deep within it
A lovely place to sleep

The Extremely Modern School Bathroom

Beneath the bathroom faucet
There's a teensy-weensy sensor
That turns the water on and off
And works the soap dispenser

The lights go on and off
By computerized switch
The hand dryer operates
By electro-thingumawich

The auto-flush toilet's great
There's just one minor issue
The toilet paper roll
Is completely out of tissue

15

Better Than Baseball

Tag is fun
Kickball's nice
You've tried soccer
Once or twice

Baseball's great
You can't deny it
You've never golfed
But want to try it

Yet none are nearly as cool for you
As lying in wet grass
Putting bugs and worms in your pockets
And bringing them back to class

The Tastiest Taste

The tastiest taste
According to some
Is the taste of
Pre-chewed bubble gum

Other people claim
That sucking on your hair
Or nibbling your fingernails
Are tastes beyond compare

Some folks shout out loud
That the tastiest taste is sugar

And then there are those who simply propose
That the tastiest taste is a booger

It's Time for Homework

Little League comes first, of course
Then dinner and dessert

A couple of cartoons
Surely will not hurt

You play an online game, just one
Make sure your hamster's fed

Now it's time for homework
Too late! It's time for bed

Snakes on the Loose!

Just before lunchtime
All the snakes got loose
You tried to get them back
But it wasn't any use

Now they slither through the pipes
Where you can't detect them
Then they pop up in a toilet
When you least expect them

They uncoil from the ceiling
And snatch the teacher's pen
Rummage through her pockets
Then coil up again

They've hacked the school computer
They've e-mailed all their kin
A million more snakes
Will soon be dropping in

Teacher Sighting

It really weirds you out
But you're completely sure
You saw your teacher shopping
At the grocery store

Teachers live at school
Of this there is no doubt
Who unlocked the door
And let your teacher out?

What's for Lunch?

Lunch today is pizza
Pepperoni or plain
In the mood for Chinese food?
Try egg rolls or chow mein

There are two desserts to choose from
Home-baked pie or muffin
Eat one or eat them both
As much as you can stuff in

grumble
grumble

This is Teacher Lunch, of course
For children's hunger cravings
The lunchroom serves recycled stuff
Like pencil sharpener shavings

They also serve dessert to kids
That looks a lot like fudge
Sniff it if you dare
It's fish tank filter sludge

The Worst Smell of All

Worse than the smell of your armpit
(A smell that many people fear)
Than the smell of the tuna sandwich
Kept in your desk for a year

Worse than the smell of a class full of kids
After recess when they sweat
When none of the windows open
And their tummies are, well, upset

Worse than the smell of Grandpa's socks
Than the smell of Dracula's tomb
Than the smell of zombie underwear
Is the smell of your teacher's perfume

You Really Wanted to Do Your Homework, but...

Mom made you make your bed
Mom made you do the dishes

Mom made you put your clothes away
Mom made you feed your fishes

Mom made you turn the TV off
And put away your game
So you had no time for homework
And your mother is to blame

Show-and-Tell Surprise

You found them in a glass
Near a little tube of gel
You've taken them to class
For weekly show-and-tell

Final Word

So you've read this book of poems
All about your school
(Or perhaps you've been asleep
And the book is soaked in drool)

So you've read this book of poems
Did you love it? Did you hate it?
(Or perhaps your dog got hold of it
To tell the truth, she ate it)

So you've read this book of poems
Did they knock you to the floor?
Did they poke you? Did they joke you?
Well, that's just what they were for